The Message

Praise for Storyshares

"One of the brightest innovators and game-changers in the education industry."
– Forbes

"Your success in applying research-validated practices to promote literacy serves as a valuable model for other organizations seeking to create evidence-based literacy programs."
- Library of Congress

"We need powerful social and educational innovation, and Storyshares is breaking new ground. The organization addresses critical problems facing our students and teachers. I am excited about the strategies it brings to the collective work of making sure every student has an equal chance in life."
– Teach For America

"It's the perfect idea. There's really nothing like this. I mean, wow, this will be a wonderful experience for young people."
- Andrea Davis Pinkney, Executive Director, Scholastic

"Reading for meaning opens opportunities for a lifetime of learning. Providing emerging readers with engaging texts that are designed to offer both challenges and support for each individual will improve their lives for years to come. Storyshares is a wonderful start."
- David Rose, Co-founder of CAST & UDL

The Message

Emily Sherwood

A Storyshares book

Storyshares

Story Share, Inc.

24 N. Bryn Mawr Avenue #340

Bryn Mawr, PA 19010-3304

www.storyshares.org

Inspiring reading with a new kind of book.

Interest Level: Middle School

Grade Level Equivalent: 1.5

9781642611984

Book design by Storyshares

Storyshares Presents

Chapter One

I DIDN'T WANT TO see my dad. I hated him for what he had done to me. But Miss Myrtle made me go.

"I know this is hard for you," she said, smiling. Miss Myrtle was always smiling. She probably smiled at her birth seventy years ago. "But remember, your parents love you. And I think you love them, too. You just may not feel that way right now."

She was right. I did not feel like loving them. Not after what they had done to me.

My family was different than most families. It was just my parents and me. We traveled all around the world together. My parents said they were security experts. It was their first lie of many.

I liked living that way, though. I had friends all over the world. I could talk to people in four languages. I had visited McDonald's in fifty countries. I never, ever got bored. It was a great way to live. Until it all ended, suddenly.

We were going through security at the airport one day. We had tickets for Spain. We were going to the Running of the Bulls. I was excited.

We took off our shoes. We went through the scanners. We stopped to put our shoes back on. Two men in suits ran toward us. A whole bunch of security guards were with them.

What happened next is still a blur. I don't remember everything. One of the men in suits opened up Mom's carry-on. He took out a picture. He looked behind the frame and nodded. And then both Mom and Dad were in handcuffs. They were being taken away.

The picture was a famous painting. My parents stole it from the Smithsonian Museum. They weren't security experts. They were thieves.

It wasn't their first theft, either. People were looking for them all over the world. I was fourteen and I'd never guessed.

So here I was now, visiting them. They were at this prison in Virginia.

Miss Myrtle said I was lucky. Most kids didn't get to see their parents in prison. They were too far away. My parents were in different buildings at the same prison. I had a foster home nearby. I could still see them.

I didn't feel lucky. The prison was scary. There were guards everywhere. A guard had to pat me down. Then she walked me to a room. It had a glass window. Dad would be on the other side.

"Your dad will be here in a minute," she said. She pointed to a telephone on the wall. "He will talk with you on that."

I nodded. That was how it worked with Mom, too. Except she just cried instead of talking. After a few minutes, she asked to leave. It was too hard for her to see me.

Dad came in, wearing an orange jumpsuit. He picked up the phone on the wall. I did, too.

"My Sienna," he said. "I've missed you so much. Do you like where you live? Is the home nice?"

I nodded. "It's OK."

"Good. I want to tell you something. I am so sorry. We never meant to hurt you."

"Then why did you?" I asked.

Dad just sat there. "We... We just did. If I could change things—"

"But you can't," I said.

That was enough. I didn't want to talk to him anymore. I hung the phone up. The guard returned.

"I'm ready to go," I said.

The guard nodded. We walked back to the lobby.

Denzel and Miss Myrtle were waiting for us. They looked up, surprised. They expected to have to wait much longer.

Denzel had been to see his dad. He was smiling. He liked visiting his dad. I didn't understand it. His dad was a drug dealer. He had never been there for Denzel.

"How was your visit?" Miss Myrtle asked, grinning.

I wanted to wipe that smile off her face. No one should be that happy all the time.

"Short," I said.

I began walking out the door. Miss Myrtle and Denzel followed.

Something flew at us from the sky. I picked it up. A paper airplane. But it had some kind of message on it. Dots.

I stuffed it in my jeans pocket. I would show it to Denzel. He knew more about prisons than I did. Denzel had been visiting the prison since he was seven. He might know what it was.

For now, I just wanted to leave.

Chapter Two

I CAME HOME TO excitement. Miss Marjorie had burned dinner. She was all upset.

She said she couldn't be a good foster mom. We all had to calm her down. Miss Myrtle said she burned toast all the time. Denzel said at least Marjorie fed us. His mom was always too stoned. I said my Mom never tried to cook. It was true. We always ate out.

Marjorie eventually calmed down and we went out to dinner. We ate Chinese. I used chopsticks and tried to teach Miss Marjorie and Denzel.

It didn't work, but was kind of interesting. And I didn't think about my parents the whole time.

I remembered the paper when we got back from dinner. I went into the kitchen. Denzel was playing Candy Crush on his tablet. Miss Marjorie had found it at a thrift shop. The screen was broken, but it worked. Denzel loved it.

"What is this?" I put the paper in front of Denzel and sat down.

Denzel looked at the paper. He scrunched his face up. "It looks like Morse Code.

"Show me the tablet," I said. "We can look—"

"No," Denzel said. "I know how to decode it."

I stared at Denzel. Miss Marjorie's eyes were bad. She sometimes couldn't read small print, like newspaper ads. I had to read it for her. Denzel couldn't. He couldn't read well enough. But he knew Morse Code?

"My Dad taught it to me, OK?" he said. "Once when he was out on bail. He knew he would go back to prison. The guards look at the mail before it goes out. He didn't want them reading his letters to me.

I nodded. It sort of made sense.

"The thing is, he writes easy stuff. He's not much better at reading than me. I can change the code and spell the letters for you. I need you to write them out," he said.

In ten minutes we had a message. The problem was, it still made no sense.

1 of 3
Heart of the State
In the Place of Gardens From Cyclops.

"What does it mean?" Denzel asked.

I shook my head. "It's a kind of riddle."

"It must be part of a series. Message one of three," Denzel said.

I nodded. "Yes, but 'Heart of the State?' What is that supposed to mean?"

"A capital!" Denzel said. "You know, where a government is for a state."

"It makes sense. But the 'Place of Gardens?'"

"New Jersey!" Denzel exclaimed.

I jumped. I didn't think Denzel could be this loud or this smart.

"It's the Garden State. We learned all the state nicknames in Social Studies."

"OK," I said. "Now. 'From Cyclops.' That is harder."

Denzel shrugged. "I have no idea."

A thought came into my head. "A cyclops is a one-eyed monster. The paper came from the prison. The entrance backs up to the exercise yard. What if a prisoner was trying to tell us something?"

"We walk by the exercise yard," Denzel said. "There's an electric fence, but it looks wooden."

I nodded. I remembered it.

"And there's a dude in the prison with one eye," Denzel said. "His other eye is glass. His name's Walker. Dad talks about him."

"What did he do?" I asked.

"He was a smart guy. He worked with numbers."

"A banker?" I asked.

Denzel nodded. "Dad says he was rich. Then he got caught. He was stealing other people's money."

"That's him, then! But why did he send us a message? Why didn't he just talk to his lawyer?" I asked.

"Dad says he's broke now. The government took his money. He has a government lawyer, like Dad. They don't help you much. And his family won't talk to him. Dad says they send back his letters."

I nodded. Everything made sense. "It's Trenton, New Jersey," I said. "It's the state capital. What should we do to get the next message?"

"We need to show him we know about it. And that we believe him," Denzel said.

"Why don't we send him a postcard? From Trenton, New Jersey? We can print one from the Internet. We can sign it 'a friend' or whatever. The guards will think it's weird. But I think Cyclops will get it."

"Then we wait until visiting day, Thursday." Denzel smiled.

I nodded my head. "We'll be like spies!" I said.

"I bet he's innocent!" said Denzel. "He has evidence to set him free. He just needs someone to help him!"

I smiled. My parents may be thieves. But I am not like them. I want to be a hero.

Chapter Three

WE SENT THE POSTCARD to the prison the next day. And we waited until Thursday.

I made it through visits with Mom and Dad. No screaming or crying by anyone. I guess that's progress.

Denzel and I walked slowly when we got outside. We didn't want to miss the next message. Miss Myrtle, as usual, didn't notice anything different.

"The trees are so nice and green," she said. "But fall colors are better."

I had heard it all before. Miss Myrtle had a thing about fall.

"Fall is so nice here," she went on.

I saw something white fly by. The message. It landed in the bun on Miss Myrtle's head.

She just kept walking. "And it is still warm in September," she said.

I hoped the paper would fall out. But it was in tight. I motioned to Denzel. He just shrugged.

"Miss Myrtle," I interrupted her. "I... ugh..." I had an idea, but it was gone.

"There's money on the ground!" said Denzel.

Miss Myrtle looked at the ground. "Where is it?"

Denzel quickly got the airplane. He put it in his pocket.

"Oh, sorry, it's just a leaf. My bad," Denzel said.

Miss Myrtle went on talking.

After dinner, Miss Marjorie went to watch TV. "Who wants to watch Jeopardy?" she asked.

She expected me to say I did. I knew all the geography answers. But I told her no. Surprised, she shuffled into the living room.

"What do we have?" I asked Denzel.

He spelled out the message.

Place of Exchange
Trinity-Chimera-End Dragon
Location in next message

"Place of exchange," I said. "Either a bank or a customs house."

"What about the words?" Denzel asked. "Trinity means three, right?"

I looked at him. Denzel was really smart. Even if he couldn't read well.

"Right. And I saw a statue of a chimera once. It is a monster with five heads. So the words are numbers. Three and five. But what about End Dragon?"

We thought for a minute.

"Revelation," Denzel said.

"What?"

"The dragon, in the book of Revelation. From the Bible. He has seven heads."

"OK." It was weird, but it worked. "So 357. Somewhere in Trenton, New Jersey."

"I don't think it's an address. There is no street name. So what does that mean?"

"What if it's a box?" Denzel said. "You know, where people put important things. Like Miss Marjorie has at the bank."

"A safe deposit box!" I said. "That would make sense. They are in banks. Trenton is a state capital. There have to be lots of banks there."

"It must be in the last message, then," Denzel said.

"Must be," I said.

"We'll know next week," Denzel said. "What should we send Walker?"

"A picture of a bank," I said. "We'll sign it 'the gardeners.'"

"Works for me," Denzel said. "Hey, Sienna?"

"Yes?" I asked.

"I'm sorry about what happened to you. To your parents. But I like working with you on this."

"Me too," I said.

This foster care thing was not so terrible after all.

Chapter Four

I was ready to go to the prison on Thursday. I was still mad. But it was getting easier to live this life. My anger was slowly going away.

"It was selfish, what we did," Mom said. "We had enough money. But we wanted the thrill."

I kind of understood that. Getting the messages was thrilling. But Denzel and I were there to help, not hurt. That was the difference.

"Was it worth it?" I asked Mom.

"Of course not," Mom said. "We lost you. You are worth more than any painting. We just... didn't think." The tears came back again. I almost felt bad for her. Almost. "Now, I just want you to know the truth. The truth is important."

The paper airplane came easy this time. It was already in a flower pot. There was a key, too. I put both of them in my pocket.

It was hard to sit through dinner. I was thinking about the message. Miss Marjorie talked on and on. "The begonias at the library were so pretty."

This town was too into flowers.

Miss Marjorie finally went to watch TV. I pulled the code out. Twenty minutes later, we sat, stumped and confused.

Near the blue and white.
Same street as the waterfront.
Gate to the republic.

I put down the tablet. "Trenton has a river. But nothing else fits. No sports teams have blue and white colors. And I am clueless about the gate."

"Is there an airport nearby?

"Not in Trenton," I said. "Do you have ideas?"

Denzel shook his head. "I'm stumped. What should we do?"

"We can send a message," I said.

"No, we can't," Denzel said. "Dad told me Walker got in trouble today. He is in solitary, by himself. He can't get mail. He must have thrown the airplane before he went."

"So we're stuck," I said.

"We're stuck," Denzel agreed.

"We've come so far," I said. "And this is it."

"For now," Denzel said. "Just for now."

But I didn't like it.

Chapter Five

I WAS IN A bad mood the next day. Not just because we didn't get the message. I also had to see Victor.

Victor was my counselor. Miss Myrtle made me see him. He was supposed to make me feel better. But he only made me annoyed.

"You look depressed," he said. "What's causing you to be blue?"

"Well, let's see. My parents are in prison. They lied to me my whole life. Wouldn't you be depressed, too?"

"I know it is hard for you. Just remember how lucky you are," he said. Him and Miss Myrtle and my luckiness. "You get to see your parents. You have a nice foster mother and foster brother."

I nodded. "They are pretty awesome."

"And you live in a nice house. Some children are homeless." Victor frowned.

"It's nice," I said. "It's not the White House or anything."

A light bulb went on in my head. That was it!

Victor said something about trust and letting go. I just nodded my head. I was too excited to think.

Miss Myrtle dropped me off afterwards. Denzel and Miss Marjorie were planting flowers. I rushed up to them.

"I've got it!" I said.

"Got what?" Miss Marjorie said.

"I know what the last message says!" I said.

"What message?" Miss Marjorie asked.

"I will tell you about it!" I said. "Miss Marjorie, we need your help. We need to go to Washington, DC!"

Chapter Six

"I UNDERSTAND WHAT HAPPENED," said Miss Marjorie. We were at the table. Denzel and I had just told her about the message. "But why Washington, DC?"

"Yeah, whatever happened to New Jersey?" Denzel asked.

"The bank is on New Jersey *Avenue,*" I said.

Blank stares.

"Washington has a bunch of streets named after states. The White House is on Pennsylvania. There is a big building on New Jersey Avenue. I remember it. It is called the Federal Gateway. "

"Federal means national," Denzel said. "Gate to the republic!"

"Right!" I said. "And it's on *New Jersey Avenue.*"

"At the US Capitol!" Denzel said. "Here, a state means a country!"

"Yes. And the building is near the river!" I said.

"It's near Navy Pier! The blue and white!"

"There must be a bank in the building," Miss Marjorie said.

I took Denzel's tablet. Quickly, I typed "Federal Gateway bank" on Google.

"There's a Capital One in the building," I said. "That's it!"

"We have the key to box 357!" Denzel said. "Miss Marjorie, we have to go to Washington!"

Miss Marjorie sighed. "It's five hours away. A lot of money in gas. And food. And we would need a hotel." She paused. "But this is important, isn't it?"

"Walker may be innocent," I said. "It's very important."

"OK," Miss Marjorie said. "We can go for a night. But no expensive city restaurants! No expensive tours!"

"I'll pack our food myself!" I said. I gave Miss Marjorie a hug. She was surprised. I didn't give many hugs. "This is going to be amazing!"

Chapter Seven

GETTING TO WASHINGTON WAS easy. We left on a Friday. We stayed in Arlington, Virginia on Friday night. On Saturday, we went into the city. There was not much traffic. It was a clear day.

"This place is awesome!" Denzel said. He was looking at the buildings.

"It was my favorite US city," I said. *Was.* Now it reminded me of my parents.

"We will drive around after the bank," Miss Marjorie said. "I think this is it!"

She parked in front of a huge, glass building.

Denzel and I almost ran through the doors. We found the bank easily.

I ran up to the counter. "We need to open a box!" I almost yelled at the teller.

"We have a key!" Denzel said.

The teller giggled. Beside us, Miss Marjorie rolled her eyes. "Teenagers," she said.

"I have one of those," the teller said. "Come with me."

We went into a big room. There were boxes all along the wall. The teller showed us where 357 was.

"I'll leave you here," she said.

We thanked her. She walked away.

"Who wants to open the box?" Miss Marjorie asked.

"My hands are shaking," I said.

"Mine, too," Denzel said. "Why don't you open it, Miss Marjorie?"

"You want me to?" Miss Marjorie asked. "But you figured out the code. You solved the riddles."

"We couldn't do this without you," I said.

"OK," Miss Marjorie said. She took a breath. Slowly, she turned the key.

"What if it's a bomb?" she stopped and whispered.

"It's not a bomb," I said.

"How do you know?" Miss Marjorie asked. "It could be anything."

I hadn't thought about that. It didn't seem likely. But still.

"Walker has been in prison for three years," I said. "Bombs only last two years or less. No bomb." Blank stares.

"I saw an exhibit on it once," I said.

"OK," Marjorie said. She closed her eyes and turned the key.

We peered in. Papers. Lots and lots of papers. She took them out.

"Letters," she said. "Just letters." We moved to a table and sat down.

"No photographs?" I asked.

"No video?" Denzel asked.

"No. Just letters."

Marjorie passed out the letters. I looked at one. It was handwritten.

Dear Katie,

I am so sorry I hurt you. It is time you know the truth. I am guilty. Very guilty. I was wrong. Very wrong. I love you. I don't expect you to forgive me. I just want you to understand. I never meant to hurt you.

Love,

Dad

"It's for his daughter," I said. "His family wouldn't talk to him. So he left letters here."

Denzel nodded. "We need to take them to his family," he said. "We'll have to find them."

"It's all the same," I said. Tears formed in my eyes.

"What's all the same?" Miss Marjorie asked.

"All this. The bad and lying parents. They think it is OK." I looked at Denzel. "Is it OK that your mom overdosed? Or that your dad got her hooked on drugs? Is it OK that I am an orphan now? I mean, I like living with you, Miss Marjorie. But it's not the same."

"I understand," said Miss Marjorie. "But I don't think that's what this means. It's not OK. I think he just wants to say he's sorry. He wants his family to understand that. Your parents do, too."

"It takes time," Denzel said. "I used to hate my dad. It was so unfair. Didn't he think about me? Didn't he know his actions would hurt me?"

I saw tears in Denzel's eyes.

"But then I realized," he said. "He didn't think about it then. He was selfish. But now he knows. And it hurts him. Even more than it hurts me. I carry his hurt when I carry that hate."

"I don't want to hate my parents," I said.

"I know," Denzel said. "And someday you won't."

Professional counseling has nothing on the honesty of a foster child.

Chapter Eight

IT TOOK A LITTLE while to find Walker's family.

The prison wouldn't let us visit him. His lawyer didn't care.

Finally, I Googled him. I found an interview with his wife. She said she was moving. She and the kids were going to Beaufort, South Carolina. Her mother lived there.

Mom and Dad did a "job" in Beaufort. I had friends there. It is a small town. I called and found the wife. Two weeks later, we drove there. We sat on a porch and drank lemonade.

"It is not fair," Katie said. She was Walker's daughter. She was fifteen. "It was so embarrassing."

"We had to leave everything," Patrick said. He was thirteen. "We lost all our money. It was hard on Mom." He looked at Mrs. Walker. She had bags under her eyes. "I hate my dad."

"I hated my parents, too," I said. "And I still am mad at them. But it gets easier. Your dad was wrong. He hurt you. But hating him hurts more."

I looked at Denzel. He smiled at me.

"He's still your dad," I said. "He still loves you."

Patrick just nodded. "It has to get better."

I nodded. "It does."

Hate is a strange thing. You think it will make you feel better. It really hurts you. It hurts you badly. Sometimes it is best to let it go.

That is what I learned from the messages. They were for Walker's family, true. But they were also for me.

About the Author

Emily Sherwood is a writer and educator in East Tennessee. When not traveling the world or advocating for education, she teaches English as a Second Language in a rural school system.

About the Publisher

Story Shares is a nonprofit focused on supporting the millions of teens and adults who struggle with reading by creating a new shelf in the library specifically for them. The ever-growing collection features content that is compelling and culturally relevant for teens and adults, yet still readable at a range of lower reading levels.

Story Shares generates content by engaging deeply with writers, bringing together a community to create this new kind of book. With more intriguing and approachable stories to choose from, the teens and adults who have fallen behind are improving their skills and beginning to discover the joy of reading. For more information, visit storyshares.org.

Easy to Read. Hard to Put Down.

Notes